TWO of a kind™
Diaries

Win a
trip to the
premiere of
Mary-Kate
and Ashley's
movie
NEW YORK MINUTE!
Details inside.

Look for more

titles:

TWO of a kind™ Diaries

Heart to Heart

by Judy Katschke
from the series created by
Robert Griffard & Howard Adler

HarperEntertainment
An Imprint of HarperCollinsPublishers
A PARACHUTE PRESS BOOK

A PARACHUTE PRESS BOOK

Parachute Publishing, L.L.C.
156 Fifth Avenue
Suite 302
New York, NY 10010

Published by
HarperEntertainment
An Imprint of HarperCollins*Publishers*
10 East 53rd Street, New York, NY 10022-5299

TWO OF A KIND books created and produced by Parachute Press, L.L.C., in cooperation with Dualstar Publications, a division of Dualstar Entertainment Group, LLC, published by HarperEntertainment, an imprint of HarperCollins Publishers.

ISBN 0-06-009329-3

HarperCollins®, ® , and HarperEntertainment™ are trademarks of HarperCollins Publishers Inc.

First printing: February 2004

Printed in the United States of America

Visit HarperEntertainment on the World Wide Web at
www.harpercollins.com

10 9 8 7 6 5 4 3 2 1

Chapter 1

Monday

Dear Diary,

I used to think Valentine's Day was a totally lame holiday. A heart-shaped box doesn't make the chocolates taste

any better, does it? And who wants a pink musical teddy bear that plays love songs? Not me. That is, until I met Jordan Marshall!

"Twelve days to go," I told my reflection in the fogged-up bathroom mirror. I stuck my toothbrush in my mouth.

Beside me my twin sister, Ashley, laughed. "Don't tell me! You're actually counting the days until Valentine's Day?"

Oops! I hadn't realized I had said those words out loud! My mouth was full of toothpaste, so I just nodded.

Cheryl Miller, Summer Sorensen, and Phoebe Cahill all glanced my way and grinned. We were crowded in front of the mirror, getting ready for the day. When you're in boarding school, you get used to sharing everything—including the bathroom!

We're all in First Form—which is what they call

the seventh grade here at the White Oak Academy for Girls in New Hampshire. At Porter House, our dorm, we share pretty much everything: clothes, makeup, shampoo, blow-dryers—and now my excitement for Valentine's Day!

"It's my first Valentine's Day with Jordan," I said. "That makes it special!"

"What about you, Ashley?" Ashley's roommate, Phoebe, asked. "Doing something special for Valentine's Day with Ross?"

Ashley's eyes lit up—like they always do whenever her boyfriend, Ross Lambert, is mentioned.

Our friends back home were surprised to hear we had boyfriends. That's because the White Oak Academy is an all-girls school. So we explained that the Harrington School for Boys is right up the road. We have classes and activities together. In fact, I met my boyfriend, Jordan, in fencing class! How swash-buckling is *that*?

Ashley's smile quickly faded. "We probably won't do anything. I should be studying for the big biology test." She sighed. "It's in four weeks."

"Four weeks?" I stared at Ashley. "And you want to start studying *now*?"

Phoebe looked surprised, too. "Didn't you just take a biology test yesterday?" she asked.

"Yes, and I'm worried about how I did," Ashley

confessed. "My grades in bio haven't been so hot lately."

I glanced at my sister's frowning face in the mirror. Her hair is the same color blond as mine. And our eyes are almost the same blue. We're alike in a lot of ways—but we're also pretty different.

Ashley likes writing, fashion design, ballet, and shopping for new clothes. I like drama, basketball, baseball—and *borrowing* Ashley's new clothes! Ashley is great in math and in English. She even writes for the First Form school paper, the *White Oak Acorn.* But for some reason she doesn't seem to get bio. When she bombed the last bio exam, it was the first time she didn't do okay on a test. And that's *not* okay with Ashley!

"Do you think you failed?" Phoebe asked.

Ashley shook her head. "No way. My grade should be pretty good," she said. "Victor Nichols in my bio class tutored me."

"Who?" Summer asked.

"He just won the science fair with his insect project," Ashley said. "Remember?"

"How can we forget?" Cheryl groaned. "Part of his project escaped and crawled all over the dining hall!"

Summer laughed. "Now I know who you mean!" She tilted her head to one side as she braided her long blond hair. "Hmm. I suppose Victor Nichols is kind of cute in a nerdy, science-geek way," she said. "But he's not exactly a hottie."

"Who cares?" Ashley said. "As long as he knows his amoebas!"

"Amoebas?" I said, wrinkling my nose.

"They're microscopic single-celled animals," Ashley explained. "They were on my last science test."

I was impressed. Ashley was learning biology!

"Is Victor going to tutor you for the next test?" Phoebe asked Ashley.

"I didn't ask him," Ashley admitted, reaching for her toothbrush. "I don't want to be a bother." She turned to me. "Why don't *you* help me study for the next test, Mary-Kate?" she asked. "You're pretty good in science."

"I'm not taking bio this semester," I reminded her. "I haven't gotten up to amoebas yet."

"Oh," Ashley said with a frown. "That's right."

"Hey," Cheryl said. "Isn't your dad a college science professor?"

Ashley and I nodded.

"Then why don't you ask *him* for help, Ashley?" Cheryl suggested.

"Are you kidding?" Ashley cried. "I can't tell my dad I'm not doing well in a subject he teaches. He'd be so disappointed."

"That's true, Ashley," I said. "But Dad will be even more disappointed if you bomb the next test."

Ashley stared at her reflection in the mirror. Then she nodded. "Okay. I'll ask Victor to tutor me."

"Good move!" I said.

"Well, now that *my* problem is solved," Ashley said, leaning on the sink, "what's everyone else doing on Valentine's Day?"

Cheryl dragged a brush through her wavy brown hair. "What I do every Valentine's Day," she said. "Watch romantic DVDs in the TV room and hope that someday they'll be about me."

"No, you won't." Phoebe tied a short scarf around her hair. "The DVD player is broken. Remember? Mrs. Pritchard made an announcement about it. She can't replace it right now because it's not in the budget."

Mrs. Pritchard is the headmistress of White Oak. Whatever she says—goes! If she says no DVD, that means no DVD.

Cheryl moaned. "And they got rid of the VCR when they got the DVD player."

"Exactly," Phoebe said.

Cheryl frowned. "This stinks!" she grumbled.

"Dateless girls at this school have been watching romantic movies on Valentine's Day for years. It's another White Oak tradition—like oatmeal for breakfast every morning."

"Don't worry, Cheryl," I said. "There'll be lots of romantic movies on TV."

"Like those amazing classic black-and-white Hollywood movies," Phoebe said. She closed her eyes, and a dreamy smile crossed her face. *"Casablanca . . . Laura. . ."*

"The 101 Dalmations!" Summer interrupted.

Cheryl stared at Summer. *"The 101 Dalmations?"*

Summer nodded. "They're black and white!"

No one said a word, but we all smiled. Summer can be a little ditzy sometimes.

"If only we could find a DVD player in time for Valentine's Day," Cheryl said. "But how? A good DVD player costs a lot of money."

"I know!" I said. "Why don't we raise some money to buy a new DVD player?"

"What a great idea!" Phoebe exclaimed. "Let's see. We can have a bake sale and bake heart-shaped cookies and cakes!"

Cheryl frowned. "I'm not sure if we could make enough money that way."

"How's this?" Ashley suggested. "Why don't we make Valentine's Day cards and sell them? We could charge more for cards than for cookies."

I rolled my eyes. "Bor-ring."

"What do you mean *boring*?" Ashley asked. "You won't say it's 'boring' if you get a Valentine's Day card from Jordan."

"What's so special about cards?" I asked. "You can buy them anywhere. No big deal."

"You're wrong," Ashley argued. "Remember that singing Valentine's Day card that Dad sent Mom when we were little?"

"Oh, yeah!" I smiled as I remembered.

Summer's eyes opened wide. "You mean the card sang and danced?" she asked.

"No!" I giggled. "It was a person dressed up as a giant Valentine's Day card. *He* sang and danced!"

"Mom got such a kick out of it," Ashley added.

Diary, I must have been on a roll, because I got the most awesome idea.

"Why don't *we* become singing Valentines?" I suggested. "We can make Cupid-y costumes, and get the girls at school to send messages or poems to the boys at Harrington they like."

"Then what?" Phoebe looked confused.

"It would be just like a singing telegram," I explained. "We put the messages to music, find the boys, and then sing our hearts out to them!"

"Hearts!" Ashley exclaimed. She began jumping up and down. "We can call ourselves . . . Heart-O-Grams!"

Everyone loved the name—and the idea! We all high-fived.

"I'll ask Mrs. Pritchard if it's okay," Ashley offered.

"Then I'll put an ad in the *Acorn*," Phoebe said. She's the editor of the First Form newspaper. "I'll make a form to fill out and send back to us with money. How does five dollars sound?"

I quickly did the math in my head.

"If about fifty girls at school send out Heart-O-Grams at five dollars each," I said, "that's two hundred and fifty dollars. We'll have enough money to buy a decent DVD player for the school."

"And I'll have movies to watch on Valentine's Day!" Cheryl cheered. "Thanks, you guys!"

Diary, I am so psyched. Not only will we raise money for a new DVD player, we'll be spreading love throughout the whole school.

And that's what Valentine's Day is all about!

Dear Diary,

Two totally awesome things happened today: My friends and I decided to become singing Valentines. And I got a B+ on my bio test!

B+—is that amazing or *what*?

You should have seen me in bio today, Diary. I stared so hard at the grade on my test that I forgot to blink!

"Keep up the good work, Ashley," Mr. Barber, the biology teacher, said to me. "If you do this well on your next exam, you'll get a good grade for the course."

And Dad will be so proud! I thought.

I knew that if I wanted to ace the next test I'd have to do two things: study hard and get Victor to tutor me again. Before Victor helped me, my grades were rock-bottom.

I quickly went over to Victor.

"Thanks for helping me pass the test, Victor," I told him. "I never expected a B plus!"

Victor looked up from his microscope to smile at me. His dark blue eyes sparkled behind his round, wire-rimmed glasses.

"You had something to do with it, too, Ashley," he said. "You did your share of studying."

"True," I said, sliding into the seat beside him. "But if I'm going to pass the next test, I'm going to need your help. Would you please tutor me again?"

"Gee, I don't know, Ashley," Victor said. "I'm kind of busy. My amoebas have been multiplying so fast. I keep having to collect new slides, stain them. . . "

Victor stopped talking. He stared at the classroom door. I followed his gaze and saw Kiara Johnson walk into the classroom.

"Did you see that?" Victor whispered.

"See what?" I asked.

"Kiara just smiled!" He whispered.

"So?" I asked. "Kiara always smiles."

I studied Kiara. Her black leather jacket and camel-colored stretch pants looked great on her. Kiara had seriously good taste. Believe me, Diary, I don't need any tutoring in fashion—and neither does she! She sat down next to her friend Jolene Dupree in the back of the room.

"This time she was smiling in my direction." Victor whispered. "That is an excellent sign."

Then Victor's cheeks began to turn red. "I mean," he blurted, "that's an excellent *smile* . . . I mean. . . "

I smiled to myself.

Aha! So that's what this was all about!

"Victor," I said. "You have a crush on Kiara Johnson, don't you?"

"Shh!" He whispered, sinking into his seat.

"Not so loud, Ashley. Don't let her hear you!"

I leaned in close to him. "But if you like Kiara so much," I said, keeping my voice low, "why don't you ask her out?"

"Because I can't talk to her without my voice cracking!" Victor groaned. "It's like that every time I try to talk to girls."

I sat straight up. "You can talk to *me*," I pointed out. "And I'm a girl."

"We usually talk about science," Victor said. "I can talk to *anyone* about science."

"Look, Victor," I said. "Kiara seems very nice. I'm sure she'd go out with a guy like you."

"Yeah, right." Victor snorted. "Kiara isn't just nice. She's *cool*. So she probably likes cool guys." He sighed. "I'm more the lukewarm type."

"Do you think if you were cooler you'd have the nerve to talk to Kiara?" I asked.

"Probably," Victor said, slumping in his chair.

He does have a point, I thought. *Victor isn't really like the cool guys in school. But that could be fixed. With the right clothes . . . the right attitude . . .*

"I have an awesome idea!" I blurted out.

"What?" Victor asked. He glanced around nervously. Okay, so maybe I had gotten a little loud. That happens when I'm enthusiastic. And this idea was truly inspired.

11

"Help me study for the next exam," I said, "and I'll help *you*!"

"Help me with what?" Victor asked.

"I'll give you a makeover so you'll be cool," I explained. "Then you'll have a better chance with Kiara."

Victor sat up straight in his chair. "Do you think it would work?" he asked.

"Sure!" I said. "I'm great at makeovers. I've helped Cheryl with her makeup. And Summer with her hair—"

"Did you ever make over a guy before?" Victor asked.

Uh-oh! I hadn't thought of that.

"We-ell," I admitted, "once when Mary-Kate and I were five, we braided our dad's hair . . . while he was sleeping. . . ."

Victor looked disappointed—a little frightened, even. Then a new idea popped into my brain.

"My boyfriend, Ross, is one of the coolest guys I know," I said. "I'm sure he'll be happy to help out!"

Mr. Barber clapped his hands for attention. But I didn't move—I needed an answer from Victor right away.

"So will you help me ace the next bio test if I help you become cool for Kiara?" I asked.

Victor glanced over his shoulder at Kiara. Then he smiled at me. "It's a deal!" We even shook on it.

So, Diary—it's all systems go!

I may not be great in biology, but I'm amazing at makeovers!

Chapter 2

Tuesday

Dear Diary,

Good news! Mrs. Pritchard gave us the thumbs-up for the Heart-O-Grams!

The only bummer is that Ashley told me this morning that she won't be able to be a singing Heart-O-Gram with us. She'll be too busy working on her bio grade—and Victor Nichols!

The rest of us are already gearing up. We have less than two weeks to spread the love—and make some money!

Yesterday Phoebe and I spent most of the afternoon designing the Heart-O-Gram costume. Today Elise Van Hook modeled it in the *Acorn* office.

"Ta-daaa!" I sang as my friends gathered to see the costume. "What every well-dressed Heart-O-Gram girl will be wearing this year!"

Elise wore a pink leotard and matching tights. A giant red cardboard heart decorated with pink and silver glitter hung over her body. We had even found her a real Cupid-style bow and arrow! She placed her hand on her hip and twirled like a supermodel.

"So cute!" Summer said.

"How did you make it?" Cheryl asked.

"Phoebe and I got the leotard from the ballet department, the cardboard heart from the art department, and the bow and arrow from the gym," I explained.

"And don't forget," Elise added with a smile, "you got the glitter from me!"

How could I forget? Elise puts glitter on practically everything—even her lip gloss!

Fiona Ferris set up her keyboard at the side of the room. Fiona is in the First Form Music Club and offered to help us make up melodies for the Heart-O-Grams. She struck a few chords as Elise went on twirling. It was like a real fashion show.

"I'll help everyone make costumes today," Phoebe said. "We want to get the Heart-O-Grams started as soon as possible."

"Wait a minute," Cheryl said. "We all have to wear that Cupid costume? On campus? Where people can see us?"

"Absolutely!" Phoebe said. "It shows that we are a team."

"And it's really cute," Summer added.

"Just keep thinking about that DVD player," I told Cheryl. "And all the great movies you'll be able to watch."

The door flew open and Valerie Metcalf walked in. Well, not exactly walked. More like, danced in.

"'We'll be swell,'" Valerie belted out. "'We'll be great." Her shiny black shoes made clicking sounds as she tap-danced across the floor. She tossed her long red hair over one shoulder.

Valerie and I are both in the Drama Club, but Valerie sings and dances even when she's not on the stage!

"Sorry I'm late," Valerie said. "I was polishing my tap shoes." She did a quick little tap step.

"You're going to sing *and* dance your Heart-O-Grams?" I asked Valerie.

"You bet!" Valerie said, her green eyes sparkling. "It will be fun!"

"Excellent," I said. This plan was really coming together!

"And look," Phoebe said, pulling a paper from the printer. "Here's the ad that's going to be in the *Acorn.* It's going out this afternoon!"

We crowded around the ad, and I read it out loud: "'Calling all girls! Now's the time to tell that crush how much you like him. For just five dollars you can send that Harrington hottie a singing Heart-O-Gram. You write the poem, and we'll sing it—anytime, anywhere!'"

We all looked up and stared at Phoebe.

"Anytime? Anywhere?" I said. "Even if it means singing 'Twinkle Twinkle, Little Star' backward? In the boys' locker room? At five o'clock in the morning?"

"Sure!" Phoebe shrugged. "What the customer wants, the customer gets! It's the only way to be really successful."

I saw Cheryl shaking her head.

"Keep thinking about that DVD player," I whispered to her.

"Why don't we do a test run?" Valerie suggested.

"What do you mean?" I asked.

Valerie pulled a piece of paper from her backpack. "Do a Heart-O-Gram for practice, just to see how it goes," she explained. "I wrote a message to my friend Alexander Broome. I know he'll think it's funny."

"That's a great idea!" Phoebe said.

Valerie handed the paper to Fiona.

Fiona studied it a minute. "Alexander Broome!" she sang as she banged on the keyboard. "You make my heart go boom!"

Everyone laughed.

Phoebe looked at Cheryl, Elise, and me. "Who wants to go first?"

Singing the first Heart-O-Gram might be fun, I thought. And the Heart-O-Gram business *was* my idea. Besides, I knew Alexander. He was in the First Form at Harrington. He was a nice guy.

"I'll do it!" I volunteered.

"That's great," Valerie said.

"But I won't tap-dance," I warned.

Elise and I hurried to the bathroom to change. She peeled off the Heart-O-Gram costume and handed it to me. In a flash I was wearing the pink leotard and tights, cardboard heart, and carrying the bow and arrow.

I looked in the mirror. The costume didn't seem weird—until it was on *me*. I looked like a giant Valentine with legs!

"You look great," Elise said. "How do you feel?"

"Like Cupid's fashion-challenged sister!" I joked.

Elise turned me toward the door and said, "Good luck. Now go out there and spread the love!"

Kids snickered and pointed to me as I made my way to the Student U. I started wondering if this was such a hot idea. *You can't back out now*, I told myself.

Valerie told me that Alexander spent his midday breaks at the White Oak U when he had classes on our campus. I looked at my watch. He should be there right now.

"Here goes," I said under my breath. I opened the door and stepped inside.

"Hey, check out Mary-Kate!" a boy called.

"I thought Halloween was over!" a girl said.

All eyes in the U were on me. My mouth felt as dry as cotton candy. But I still managed to squeak, "H-h-hi, everyone!"

I spotted Alexander Broome sitting in a beanbag chair. He was staring at me, too.

"This Heart-O-Gram is for Alexander Broome!" I announced.

I hoped no one noticed how nervous I was. I clutched the paper with Valerie's message written on it. I took a deep breath and began to sing. "Alexander Broome—you make my heart go boom!"

Alex blushed and sank even deeper into the beanbag.

I launched into the big finish. "Let's get together and have some laughs! Lovingly yours— Valerie Metcalf!"

Silence. I looked up from the note. No one said a word. Not even Alexander.

Great, I thought. *Did I just make a total fool of myself?*

Then Alex grinned. "Tell Valerie thanks," he said. "I'll e-mail her tonight."

The whole U cheered and applauded!

"Thank you, thank you!" I said, curtsying. "And, girls, look for our form in the *Acorn* this afternoon. You can send a Heart-O-Gram to the boy of *your* dreams!"

The first Heart-O-Gram in White Oak history was a huge success!

Dear Diary,

This must be my lucky day. Right before third period I found Ross heading to his next class. I asked him if he would help me with Victor's makeover.

"Sure," he said. "When it comes to the subject of cool, I'm an expert!"

We walked across campus together. I could see my breath every time I said anything. New Hampshire winters are wicked cold!

"I already have a plan, Ross," I told him. "I'm going to have Victor practice talking to girls. This way when it's time for him to talk to Kiara, he'll be a pro!"

"Good idea," Ross agreed. "I'll look through my closet for some clothes to lend Victor. He really needs help with that."

Heart to Heart

We stopped in front of the History Building. That's where my next class was.

"I really hope this works, Ross," I said. "Victor helped me so much on the last test. I never would have gotten a B plus if it weren't for him."

"I'm sure you studied hard for it," Ross said.

"That's for sure!" I declared. "After all my studying for this next exam, I'm going to need a serious break!"

"You mean like a vacation?" Ross asked.

"Exactly!" I smiled. *Vacation.* The word made me feel all warm and fuzzy inside. "Remember when we had that school trip to Hawaii over summer break? That was the best vacation ever!"

"Surfing," Ross said. His voice got dreamy. "Sailing."

"Sunshine!" I rubbed my hands together to get them warm. "Temperatures above freezing!" I stamped my feet. "Wouldn't it be great to be there right now?"

"Definitely," Ross said. He tapped the pom-pom on top of my hat. "Who knows, maybe you'll get to go back to Hawaii someday!"

"I wish!" I sighed. "Right now I have to concentrate on turning Victor into an irresistible Harrington hottie!" I giggled. "I'm actually pretty psyched about it!"

I climbed the stairs of the History Building.

"Hey, wait!" Ross called up to me. "There's something else you can start getting psyched about."

I stopped on the stairs and turned around. "Really?" I said. "What?"

"My Valentine's Day present for you!" Ross answered. "It's going to be very romantic."

I stared down at Ross. I was giving him a romantic present, too: a CD mix of hit love songs. But what was he giving me?

"What is it?" I called down the steps. "Tell me—tell me—tell me!"

"Nuh-uh," Ross said with a sly smile. "It's a surprise. And I know how much you love surprises."

He gave a little wave and jogged away.

I tried to guess what Ross's romantic Valentine surprise would be. Jewelry? Perfume? A book of love poems? Then I remembered my history class and flew up the stairs!

Diary! I'm dying to know what Ross's romantic surprise is.

But then it wouldn't be a surprise . . . would it?

Chapter 3

Wednesday

Dear Diary,

Our Heart-O-Gram ad came out in the *Acorn* yesterday afternoon. As soon as I got to the gym for fencing class, I showed it to Jordan.

"Check this out!" I said, holding up the newspaper.

Jordan slid over to me on the bleachers. He was wearing navy blue sweatpants and a white T-shirt. I had on a black leotard and gray sweatpants. They felt a lot more comfortable than a cardboard heart with glitter!

"Pretty cool, Mary-Kate," Jordan said after he read the ad. "Now check out the article on the same page."

Jordan pointed to the top half of the page. There was a whole story about him winning the big inter-school boys fencing match.

"Jordan, this is great!" I exclaimed.

"Thanks," Jordan said. "I faxed the article to my mom yesterday. She gets a kick out of that sort of stuff."

I got a kick out of it, too. Just think, Diary, not only is the champion fencer at Harrington my boyfriend, he's my fencing partner, too!

I placed my copy of the *Acorn* on the bleachers and picked up my fencing sword. Just as I was ready to practice a lunge, Coach Slotsky blew his whistle.

"Attention, s'il vous plaît!" he called.

That means "Attention, please," in French. Coach Slotsky loves to use French words even though he isn't French. I think it's because the sport of fencing began in France.

"We're switching fencing partners today," Coach announced. *"Oui?"*

That was French for "yes," but my answer was definitely no!

I didn't want a new fencing partner—I wanted Jordan. My hand shot up in the air.

"Coach Slotsky?" I blurted out. "Can Jordan and I stay partners? We're sort of a . . . team."

"You mean a couple!" Trevor Apfelbaum snickered. He pursed his lips and began making kissing noises.

I glared at obnoxious Trevor. Why did he have to be in this class?

I turned back to Coach. I tried to send him thought waves to get him to agree.

He shook his head. "Sorry. *C'est la vie.*"

"Huh?" I said.

"I think that's French for 'forget it,'" Jordan whispered.

Coach read out our new partners: "Seth Samuels and Lexy Martin. Molly Chin and Anita Alverez. Jordan Marshall and Mena Morris . . . "

"Mena," I repeated to myself. Mena was sitting on the bottom row of the bleachers. She turned and gave Jordan her usual one-hundred-watt smile.

"Hey," Jordan said, waving at Mena.

Then I heard Coach call out *my* name.

"Mary-Kate Burke and . . ."

And? And? And?

"Trevor Apfelbaum."

Diary, my mouth must have dropped about a mile. I would rather fence with Captain Hook than with creepy Trevor Apfelbaum!

"Yo, Mary-Kate," Trevor called. He whipped his sword in the air. "You think I've got the Zorro thing going on?"

"More like zero," I muttered.

We climbed off the bleachers and joined our new partners for the warm-up. Jordan and Mena quickly started to fence. I just frowned at Trevor.

"Okay, teams," Coach said. "Get into the ready position."

I'm never *going to be ready,* I thought. *I want to keep fencing with Jordan.*

I shook the thought out of my head. I needed all of my concentration to avoid being stabbed by Trevor!

I'd keep on writing, Diary, but the Heart-O-Gram orders are pouring in. In fact, I have a Heart-O-Gram to deliver right now!

Dear Diary,

I could hardly sit still all morning. Today was the first day of Operation Change Victor, and I was ready for action!

When lunch period finally rolled around, I raced to the dining hall to meet Victor. On Wednesdays, the guys from Harrington are allowed to eat with the girls from White Oak—as long as there aren't any food fights!

"You want me to speak to girls?" Victor squeaked when I told him my plan. "Here? Now?"

I giggled to myself. Victor's dark blue eyes behind his glasses were as round as Frisbees!

"It's great practice, Victor," I explained. "For when you start talking to Kiara!"

Victor sipped from his cranberry juice box. "Okay," he said finally. "What do I have to do?"

I nodded toward the other end of the table.

"You see those two girls over there?" I said. "Those are my friends Samantha Kramer and Wendy Linden. They're very nice."

"Are they good in science?" Victor asked. "We can talk about science—"

I cut him off quickly. "No!" I ordered. "You can talk about anything *but* science. That's your challenge!"

Victor looked worried. But then he gave me a nod and said, "Here I go."

He picked up his tray and carried it over to Wendy and Samantha. I slid over two chairs and pretended to study. But I was really listening in!

"H-h-hi," Victor blurted out. "I'm Victor."

Wendy and Samantha looked up at Victor and smiled.

"Hi. I'm Wendy."

"Samantha."

Victor plunked down his tray and sat in an empty seat. There were about fifteen seconds of silence until Wendy finally said, "The tuna fish is good today."

"Not bad," Samantha agreed.

I peeked over my book. Victor wasn't speaking.

Just nodding over and over like one of those bobble-head dolls Mary-Kate likes so much.

Say something, Victor, I thought. *Anything!*

"Uh. I hate tomatoes in my tuna sandwich," Victor said. "Gets . . . soggy."

Diary, I wanted to sink behind my book. Even the *weather* makes better conversation than soggy tomatoes!

Wendy smiled at Victor. "Hey," she said. "Aren't you the guy who's really good in science?"

"You won the science fair, didn't you?" Samantha asked.

Uh-oh, I thought. *There it is—the S word.*

At least Victor would have something to talk about, I decided. That was better than nothing!

"You bet!" Victor said. He straightened up and grinned. "My next science fair project will be on chlorophyll. Only green plants can make their own food. A plant that doesn't make its own food is called a fungus. They get their food from dead wood or from dirt with rotten plants and insects in it. . . ."

The girls stared down at their salads. Then they jumped up with their trays.

"Um," Samantha said, "I have to go to the library and return a book."

"And I have to straighten out my locker," Wendy said. "It's a mess!"

Victor sat frozen as both girls bolted from the table. I slid over to the seat next to him.

"I blew it, Ashley," Victor wailed. "Blew it!"

I patted his shoulder. "Don't worry, Victor," I said. "There's still almost two weeks before Valentine's Day to practice."

I guess some guys just need a little more help, Diary.

Or, in Victor's case—a *lot* more!

Chapter 4

Thursday

Dear Diary,

I don't get it. I had every reason to believe that this was going to be a super day.

For starters, our Heart-O-Gram business was already booming. By late afternoon, I sang five Heart-O-Grams all over campus. When I ran into Jordan after school, I was totally psyched!

"I even sang a Heart-O-Gram from Ms. Padillo, the Spanish teacher, to Mr. Verko, the art teacher!" I told him.

"Wow!" Jordan exclaimed. "What did Mr. Verko think of the gram?"

"He must have liked it." I giggled. "He gave it an A plus!"

It started to snow as we walked across campus. I was happy to be wearing my bulky black parka and scarf and not my Heart-O-Gram costume.

"I feel like celebrating," I said, wrapping my gray scarf tighter around my neck. "How about some hot cocoa at the U?"

"Can't," Jordan said, shaking his head. "I'm meeting Mena in the gym."

"Mena?" I said. "Your new fencing partner?"

"She wants to get in some practice." Jordan pretended to fence with an imaginary sword. "You should see her fence," he said. "She's really good!"

"Oh," I said.

"Got to go!" He raced toward the gym.

Sure I was bummed. But I wasn't going to let Jordan's fencing plans spoil my practically perfect day!

I guess I'll sing some more Heart-O-Grams, I decided. *While I'm on a roll!*

When I got to the *Acorn* office, the whole team was there.

"Did we raise enough money for a DVD player yet?" I asked Phoebe.

"Not yet," Phoebe replied. "But we're getting close!"

Summer pointed to a basket on Phoebe's desk. "Look at all the new orders that came in today," she said. "It's like every girl in school wants to send out a Heart-O-Gram!"

"DVD player, here we come!" Cheryl cheered.

Cheryl, Valerie, Elise, and I dug through the Heart-O-Gram basket on Phoebe's desk. We pulled out a few to read. Each of the orders had five-dollar bills clipped to them!

"Oh no," Cheryl groaned. "This person wants me to sing a poem in Italian."

"This girl wants me to sing her Heart-O-Gram standing on my head!" Elise cried. "Do you believe it?"

I unfolded a form. I blinked a few times as I read it over and over. "You guys!" I said, my voice shaky. "This Heart-O-Gram is for Jordan Marshall!"

"Your boyfriend?" Summer gasped.

"What?" Valerie said.

"Who sent it?" Phoebe demanded.

"I don't know," I said. "The person didn't fill in the 'Sent By' section."

"Read it to us," Cheryl said. "The girl's name has to be somewhere in the message."

I took a deep breath and read the Heart-O-Gram out loud: "'Dear Pookie . . .'"

"Pookie?" Cheryl said, wrinkling her nose.

"'You will always be the sunshine of my life,'" I continued. "'Stay as sweet as you are. From, You Know Who.'"

"You Know Who?" Cheryl repeated. "Who is You Know Who?"

That's what I wanted to know!

"A secret admirer!" Elise said in a hushed voice.

Heart to Heart

"Maybe there's a name on the envelope," Phoebe said. She turned to Summer. "Summer, you opened the last batch of Heart-O-Grams during midday break. What did you do with the envelopes?"

We watched Summer as she tried to remember. She frowned. "I threw them away," she admitted.

We raced to the big trash can. But the garbage had already been picked up!

"Great." I groaned. "All we know is that Jordan's Heart-O-Gram came from a You Know Who. And that she calls him P-P-P-Pookie!" I was working hard to not burst into tears.

Fiona struck a chord on her keyboard and began to sing: "Pookie, Pookie! You're sweeter than a cookie—"

"Stop!" I cried. "Someone has just written a love letter to my boyfriend. And I have no idea who she is! And the worst part is that probably Jordan *does*!"

Everyone in the office looked at me.

"Sorry," Fiona murmured.

"That's okay," I said. I knew she hadn't meant to hurt my feelings.

Got to go now, Diary. My roomie, Campbell, and I are going to watch a basketball game in the TV room. That ought to take my mind off of Jordan.

For a few seconds!

Dear Diary,

Okay, so my last try to make over Victor totally tanked. But that doesn't mean I'm about to give up!

"Why did you want to meet me in the gym?" Victor asked me during midday break. "I stink at sports!"

"Don't worry," I told him. "I brought you here for the next part of my plan."

"Which is . . . ?" Victor asked.

"Your wardrobe!" I declared.

"You mean my clothes?" He pulled off his navy-blue parka and looked himself up and down. "What's wrong with my clothes?"

I studied Victor from head to toe. He wore a stretched-out T-shirt. His jeans had frayed holes in the knees and pen marks on the pockets. His dirty sneakers may have once been white, but I wasn't sure.

"Those pants might have been cool once," I explained, "but not anymore. And that T-shirt has a stain on it."

Victor glanced down at the stain. "That was from one of my science projects," he said. "I took these live dung beetles and—"

"Spare me the details." I shuddered. "Let's start talking about new clothes."

"I can't go out and buy a whole new wardrobe!" Victor protested.

"Who said you have to?" I asked with a smile. "Ross offered to lend you some of his own clothes."

Victor's eyebrows raised. "He did?"

I spotted Ross coming into the gym carrying a shopping bag.

"Here comes Ross now," I said, waving.

Ross strolled over to us and he handed Victor the shopping bag. "Here, dude. Knock yourself out."

Victor rummaged through the bag. "Wow," he said. "Sweaters, pants, socks—"

"Socks?" I said.

"Don't worry, they're clean," Ross promised.

I grinned. Ross really had come through for us.

"Thanks for helping out, Ross," I said.

"No problem," Ross said. He gave me a quick kiss. "You know I'd do anything for you!"

Victor cleared his throat. I could tell he was getting a little embarrassed.

"Okay," I said, taking the bag. "Let's see what we've got here."

The guys watched as I dug through the clothes. I pulled out a great-looking gray sweater and an almost-new pair of black jeans.

I pressed the clothes against Victor's chest. "Go try these on. Then come out and work it."

Victor shrugged, but he disappeared into the boys' locker room.

"He's going to look great," I told Ross.

"For sure," Ross agreed. "Oh, I almost forgot. I have something for you, too."

"For me?" I said. "What is it?"

"Part of your Valentine present," Ross answered.

"*Part* of my Valentine present?" I asked. "You mean this is just the beginning?"

I watched Ross dig into his backpack. What did *part* mean? A million possibilities raced through my mind.

Was it a charm to go with a bracelet that Ross was giving me? Or a picture of us to go into a heart-shaped frame that Ross was saving for me? Or a—

"Ta-daaa!" Ross cheered.

 I stared as he pulled out a giant pair of sunglasses. Plastic palm trees sprouted out on each side.

"Here. Try them on!" Ross hooked the outrageous sunglasses over my ears. He stepped back and chuckled. "They're perfect!"

"Yeah," I said, totally confused. "Perfectly goofy."

A few kids snickered as they walked by. I quickly took them off.

"Ross?" I said. "What makes these glasses part of my Valentine present?"

"Can't tell you," Ross said. "Surprise—remember?"

I watched Ross leave the gym. I gazed down at the sunglasses and shook my head. *I just don't get it.*

The locker-room door swung open. Victor stepped out.

A brand-new Victor!

"What do you think?" he asked.

I gaped at Victor in his new outfit. "I think you look amazing!" And I meant it!

"Aren't the jeans a little too long?" Victor asked, lifting a leg. The hem completely covered his shoe.

I shook my head. "No way," I assured him. "That's the look."

Victor shrugged. "Okay, what do I do next?"

I shoved the shopping bag into Victor's hand.

"Take all these clothes back to your room," I said. "And wear that outfit tomorrow night to the Student U. Right after dinner."

Victor looked confused. "Why the U tomorrow night?" he asked.

"Because," I said slyly, "I'll make sure Kiara is there, too."

"Ohhhh." Victor nodded as the plan sunk in. Then he shook his head. "I don't know, Ashley. What if this doesn't work? What if I look okay, but when I try to talk to Kiara nothing comes out?"

"That will not happen," I said.

"How do you know?" he asked.

"Simple," I said. "If you look cool, you feel cool, and if you feel cool, you *act* cool!"

"How do you know that?" Victor asked.

I grinned. "Because I've always believed in the power of new clothes!"

And if you don't believe me, Diary, check out my closet!

Chapter 5

Friday

Dear Diary,

When I went to the dining hall for breakfast this morning, my eyes looked like spin art. I was up all night worrying about Jordan's Heart-O-Gram.

Who is You Know Who?

"I think it stinks!" Cheryl grumbled.

"What?" Elise asked. "The prune oatmeal?"

"Jordan's Heart-O-Gram!" Cheryl looked across the table at me. "Whoever sent it must know Jordan has a girlfriend."

"Maybe it was a mistake," Summer said. "Maybe there's another Jordan Marshall at Harrington."

I stirred brown sugar into my oatmeal and shook my head. "No such luck," I said. "Some girl out there likes Jordan. And, for all I know, he likes her, too."

Ashley sat across from me. Last night I had told her all about the Heart-O-Gram.

"What are you going to do, Mary-Kate?" Ashley asked. "Are you going to sing the Heart-O-Gram to Jordan?"

I almost sputtered in my oatmeal!

"Sing it to him?" I cried. "I'd rather brush my teeth with swamp water! I'd rather eat peanut butter with sardines!"

"I guess that means no," Cheryl said.

Phoebe put down her toast and faced me directly. "Someone has to sing it, Mary-Kate. We promised to sing every gram that comes in, remember?"

"How can I forget?" I muttered.

Valerie leaned over the table and patted my hand. "You know, Mary-Kate," she said, "I can always sing it for you."

"You?" I asked.

I pictured Valerie tap-dancing her way through You Know Who's Heart-O-Gram. She'd make such a big deal out of it, Jordan might be totally impressed with You Know Who—and maybe he'd even go out with her!

That's when I decided I had to be the one to deliver it!

"Thanks, Valerie," I said. "But I think I should sing the Heart-O-Gram to Jordan."

"Why?" Valerie asked.

"Because I want to see how Jordan reacts when he hears the words 'You Know Who,'" I explained.

My friends were quiet for a moment.

"Makes sense," Ashley said.

"Good luck, Mary-Kate," Summer offered.

"Thanks," I said. "I'm going to need it!"

At midday break, I changed into my costume and searched for Jordan. I found him in front of the

Heart to Heart

U, having a snowball fight with some other kids.

"Jordan!" I called. "I have a—"

WHOMP! Glitter flew everywhere as a snowball hit my cardboard heart.

"Sorry, Mary-Kate!" Jordan said as he ran over. "That was meant for Josh Weidermeyer. But he ducked!"

"It's okay," I said, brushing off the snow.

"Hey," Jordan said. He pointed to my costume. "Who are you singing to next?"

I took a deep, deep breath. Then I looked Jordan straight in the eye and said, "You!"

Jordan smiled as I belted out the song. I couldn't bring myself to sing the Pookie part, so I left it out but sang the rest. When I was finished I waited for Jordan's reaction. All he did was grin.

"Wow, Mary-Kate," Jordan said. "I didn't think you'd send me a Heart-O-Gram. That's so sweet."

"What?" I said.

Jordan thought the Heart-O-Gram was from me!

"I *didn't* send it," I said.

"Then who did?" Jordan asked, surprised.

"You Know Who did!" I answered. I pointed to the name on the message. "Which means you know

41

who she is. Who is she, Jordan? Who is You Know Who?"

"I don't know!" Jordan said, shaking his head. Then he smiled a slow smile. "Hey . . . does this mean I have a secret admirer? Cool!"

"Cool?" I couldn't believe it! He was happy that he had a secret admirer! I picked up a handful of snow.

Before I could hurl the snowball at Jordan, his hands were on my shoulders.

"I was just kidding," he said. "Besides, I really don't know who this girl is. I mean it!"

I studied Jordan's face. There was something about his big, puppy-dog eyes that told me he was telling the truth. I dropped the snowball.

"Let's just forget it." I forced myself to smile. "I have to go now, anyway."

"Do you have more grams to sing?" Jordan asked.

"No," I said, jumping up and down. "I'm freezing in these tights!"

As I hurried back to Porter House, I felt awful. No matter what I had told Jordan, I knew I wouldn't be able to forget about You Know Who.

It's not like me to be jealous, Diary! In fact, the last time I was really, really jealous was when Ashley got a nicer Pretty Little Pony than me!

And that was eight years ago!

Heart to Heart

Dear Diary,

Tonight I could hardly sit still on my beanbag chair in the U. The "new" Victor Nichols was about to make his first appearance!

Kiara was there, too, just as I'd planned. I told her I had to copy her biology notes (not true!).

"You know, Kiara," I said as I doodled in my notebook, pretending to write notes, "I never would have passed the last bio test if it weren't for Victor."

"Victor?" she repeated.

"Yes," I said. *"Victor!"*

I was about to say more when the door flew open and in walked Ross—and Victor! Not only was Victor wearing Ross's clothes, but his hair had some kind of gel in it.

"Well, what do you know?" I said, trying to act surprised. "Here's Victor now!"

Both guys swaggered into the room. Ross gave Victor a little nudge. Victor smiled and gave Kiara a wave. Then they crossed over to the beverage machine.

"Victor looks kind of different," Kiara said.

"Do you think?" I asked.

Victor popped the cap off his soda. He and Ross strolled toward us. From the corner of my eye, I noticed Kiara smiling!

It's working, I thought. *Kiara likes Victor's new look.*

"Hi, Ashley," Victor said. "Hi, Ki—eeeeee—aaaa— Whoaaaaa!"

Victor tripped over the hem of his jeans. He stumbled and lurched toward Kiara. I sprang up from my chair, but Kiara wasn't so quick.

"Eeee!" She shrieked. Victor's orange soda splashed all over her crisp white shirt!

"Omigosh!" Victor said as he straightened up. "I-I-I'm sorry, Kiara."

Kiara held her shirt away from her body and stared down at it. There was a big orange stain covering the front!

"I-I'm really sorry!" Victor said again.

"Forget it," Kiara said. She never looked up as she hurried toward the door. Her eyes were glued on the stain.

"Kiara, wait!" I called. "You forgot your bio notes!"

But it was too late. Kiara had left the U.

"Bummer," Ross said to Victor.

Victor looked straight at me. "I told you these jeans were too long, Ashley," he said.

"Um," I said, "cuffs can be cool, too."

Victor shook his head. "Don't bother, Ashley," he

said. "I should quit before I make a total jerk of myself again."

I stared at Victor. "Quit?" I gasped. "We can't quit now. We're just getting started!"

"And I'm getting *nowhere*!" Victor wailed. "Maybe I should just forget about girls completely."

He started walking away. I grabbed him by his sweater sleeve and spun him around.

"Victor!" I said. "Who would you rather spend Valentine's Day with, your amoebas . . . or Kiara Johnson?"

Victor gawked at me. "Well," he said slowly, "if you put it that way . . ."

He promised not to quit. And I promised to think of a new plan that was sure to work.

"Then we'll study for the bio test, okay?" I called after Victor as he headed toward the door.

Victor nodded as he left the U.

"Boy, that was close," I told Ross. "Victor almost gave up."

"Maybe he should have," Ross said.

"What? Why?" I asked.

"Because maybe this is a waste of time," Ross explained. "Victor isn't exactly cool material."

I shook my head. "I made a promise to help Victor, and I'm going to keep it. Besides, I still need him to help me study. We made a deal."

Ross shrugged. "If you say so." He reached into his pocket. "Before I forget, I brought something for you. Close your eyes and hold out your hand."

"Another surprise?" I asked.

I squeezed my eyes shut and held out my hand. The goofy glasses were probably just a joke! This had to be the real thing. The real *romantic* thing!

I felt something small and hard drop into my palm. A tiny perfume bottle? A pendant?

"Open your eyes!" Ross said.

I glanced down at my palm and gulped. It wasn't perfume and it wasn't a pendant. It was some kind of tiny . . . log!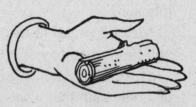

"Surprise!" Ross declared. "It's another part of your Valentine's present!"

"What is it?" I asked.

"Put it in a glass of water until it sprouts roots," Ross explained. "Then plant it in soil and watch it grow."

"It's a . . . plant?" I asked.

"An *exotic* plant!" Ross corrected. "You'll see. It's very romantic."

It didn't look romantic to me. But as Dad always taught Mary-Kate and me, it's the *thought* that really counts. I just wish I could figure out exactly what Ross was thinking!

"It's great, Ross. Thanks," I said. "I can't wait to see the rest of my present. Whatever it is."

As I carried the weird little plant back to my dorm, I couldn't stop wondering: Do Ross and I have the same idea about *romance*?

Diary, I don't think so!

Chapter 6

Tuesday

Dear Diary,

It's Saturday, and that means a whole day of Heart-O-Grams. But no one on Team Heart-O-Gram would deliver their love notes until they got the whole Jordan scoop!

"Come on, Mary-Kate—give," Cheryl said in the *Acorn* office. "Did the name Pookie ring a bell with Jordan?"

"I skipped that part," I admitted. "I couldn't get the word out of my mouth."

Valerie straightened her cardboard heart. "You know what you have to do now, don't you?" she asked.

"No. What?" I asked.

"You have to find out who You Know Who is!" Valerie said. "Once and for all."

Elise and Cheryl nodded in agreement.

"No, I don't," I insisted. "If it doesn't matter to Jordan, it doesn't matter to me."

Okay, Diary, that wasn't the total truth—but I *wanted* to feel that way!

"Yeah, right," Valerie scoffed. "It may not matter yet. But what if the Heart-O-Gram was just the *first* step?"

I stared at Valerie. "What do you mean . . . first step?"

"What if You Know Who starts *flirting* with Jordan next?" Valerie asked.

"And finding ways to spend time with him?" Cheryl suggested.

"Until," Valerie said, "she asks him out on a date. And Jordan's secret admirer isn't a secret anymore!"

I stared at Valerie, Cheryl, and Elise, one after the other. What if they were right? What if I hadn't seen the last of You Know Who—whoever she was?

"Hate to break this up," Phoebe said, handing out Heart-O-Gram requests. "But we have other people's love lives at stake. Not to mention our DVD player!"

Fiona taught us some tunes, and we scattered. As I walked to my first assignment, all I could think about was You Know Who. There were hundreds of girls at White Oak. How could I ever figure out which one was Jordan's secret admirer?

My first gram was at the Saturday Classic Comic Collectors Club. It was for a guy named Louie from a girl named Tracy.

When I walked in, the comic club was busy reading comics about superheroes and weird creatures with three heads. As soon as they saw me they went wild.

"Aaaah!" one boy screamed in pretend horror. "It's the attack of the Heart-O-Gram!"

"Great tights!" a girl called out. "They're so—Wonder Woman!"

I plastered a big smile on my face. "This Heart-O-Gram is for Louie Manzini," I announced.

"Yo, Lou-ie!" a boy teased.

"Oh, man!" A dark-haired boy groaned and covered his face with his comic book. I figured he must be Louie.

"Lou, Lou—there's no one like yooou!" I sang.

My eyes darted around the room. They landed on a girl named Renee. I remembered that Renee made Jordan a leather bracelet that he wears all the time.

Could Renee be You Know Who?

"I hope that I'm your sweetheart-to-be . . . love and kisses—Renee!"

Total silence.

"Renee?" Louie repeated, stunned.

Uh-oh! I was so busy thinking about Renee that I sang *her* name instead of Tracy's! And it didn't even rhyme.

Louie didn't seem to mind. He wasn't embarrassed anymore. Now he was flashing Renee a huge smile.

"Wow, thanks, Renee!" Louie said. "All this time I wanted to ask *you* out!"

A girl stood up and planted her hands on her hips. Her cheeks were red. "Oh, really?" she demanded. "*I* sent you that Heart-O-Gram, Louie. Now I'm sorry I did!"

Ooops. That must be Tracy, I thought.

"But I don't like Louie!" Renee protested. "I mean—I like him—but—I don't like him *that* way!"

Diary, I wanted to disappear!

Not only did I sing out the wrong name, I sang the name of the girl that Louie *really* liked. Only she didn't like him back!

"I'm sorry, you guys!" I pleaded. "I meant to say Tracy—not Renee. Let me sing it again, please!"

"Don't bother," Tracy said. She held her hand out to me. "I want my five dollars back!"

Boy, Diary, did I mess up! And I know the reason why.

I have You Know Who on the brain!

Dear Diary,

It was two o'clock on a Saturday afternoon and Victor was studying in the library. Big surprise!

I slammed shut his book on the wonders of gypsy moths and dragged him outside.

"Why are we out here, Ashley?" Victor asked. "It's less than thirty degrees!"

I only let go of his jacket sleeve when we arrived at the field behind the Main Building. It seemed like the whole school was having a blast in the snow.

"My latest plan," I announced.

I scanned the scene and spotted Kiara in her fuzzy white jacket and matching hat. She practically blended in with the snow. She was building a snowman with her friend Alyssa Fuji.

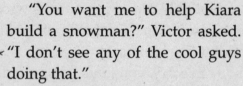

"You want me to help Kiara build a snowman?" Victor asked. "I don't see any of the cool guys doing that."

"No." I pointed to a group of kids snowboarding down a hill. "I want you to do *that*!"

"Snowboard?" Victor gasped. "I've never even stood on a snowboard. It's so . . . extreme!"

"It's easy once you get the hang of it," I said. "And most important, it's what all the cool guys on campus are doing these days."

Ross trudged over to us. He had his own snowboard tucked under his arm. "Hey, Victor," he said. "What's up?"

Ross tried rapping knuckles with Victor. But Victor kept missing.

I guess I'll have to work on that, too, I thought.

"Ashley asked me to show you the ropes," Ross said, patting his snowboard.

"You mean you're going to teach me?" Victor asked.

"Sure." Ross shrugged. "All you need are the basics. You'll be snowboarding like a pro in no time."

"My job will be to point you out to Kiara as you snowboard down the hill," I said.

Victor glanced at Kiara. She was tying a striped scarf around the snowman's neck.

"I'll give it a shot," Victor agreed. "I'm a fast learner."

"Break a leg!" I called as Ross led Victor up the hill. "I mean–good luck!"

I watched them stop at the top of the hill. Ross pointed to the snowboard. Victor nodded as if he understood. Then he jumped on top of the board.

Victor is a fast learner, I thought. *I'd better work fast, too!*

"Nice snowman you've got there," I said as I joined Alyssa and Kiara.

"Thanks," Kiara said. "Alyssa wants it to look like Mr. Salazar, the history teacher."

"He is so hot!" Alyssa giggled.

But I wasn't there to talk about snowmen or history teachers. I was there to talk about Victor!

"Hey, Kiara," I said. "Isn't that Victor up on the hill?"

"Victor?" Kiara stopped working on the snowman to turn around. Her mouth dropped wide open, and I saw why.

Victor was racing down the hill on Ross's snowboard. His arms flapped up and down. His body rocked back and forth. And he was zooming right toward us!

"Look out below!" Victor shouted. "I can't stop!"

The three of us scattered in different directions. The snowman exploded as Victor crashed into it.

"Oh, no!" Alyssa groaned. "Look what he did to Mr. Salazar!"

Big chunks of snow fell off Victor as he sat up. "Um," he said. "H-h-hi, Kiara!"

Kiara mumbled "Hi" under her breath. She and Alyssa brushed snow off each other. She grabbed her scarf, and then they hurried away.

"I messed up again, Ashley!" Victor wailed. "What am I going to do now?"

I didn't have a clue. But no way could I admit that to Victor! I had to make him believe I had it all under control.

"You have snow all over your glasses," I said, buying some time to come up with a new idea. "Let me give you a tissue."

I reached into my backpack and spotted the latest issue of *Teen Scream* magazine. That gave me another idea!

"Victor!" I said. "I know what you have to do next."

"No, thanks," Victor said. He frowned as he stood up. "I'd rather go study my amoebas."

"Oh, no, you don't!" I said. "Study this for a change!"

I shoved the magazine into Victor's hands.

"*Teen Scream*?" he said, looking at it. "I never read this stuff."

"It's time you did," I declared. "It's full of articles on what celebrity guys do, wear, and say."

Victor flipped through the magazine.

"There's even an interview with Matt Clerc about his favorite pizza," I added.

"Who's Matt Clerc?" Victor asked.

"Victor, get with it!" I shook my head. "He's just the hottest teen celeb around!"

Victor looked at me blankly. "Oh."

"And start watching television," I added.

"I do already," Victor said. "*Biology Now* is my favorite show."

I opened and shut my mouth. Instead of saying anything, I gave Victor a list of Saturday-afternoon teen shows to watch. I told him it was his homework assignment.

"How am I going to remember all this cool stuff by Valentine's Day?" Victor asked. "That's a week away!"

"Take notes," I suggested. "Pretend you're studying for a test. You're great at studying, right?"

"As I said," Victor said, "I'm a fast learner."

Diary, he'd *better* be a fast learner. Because I'm running out of ideas!

Chapter 7

Sunday

Dear Diary,

Last night there was a special White Oak and Harrington ice-cream sundae party. It started out great. Especially when Ross said he had another present for me. I was thrilled. Could *this* be the romantic surprise I was hoping for?

Ross smiled as he reached into his pocket. His eyes gleamed as he slowly pulled out . . .

"A lizard!" I gasped.

That's right, Diary—a lizard!

"It's really a rubber gecko!" Ross laughed. He held the wiggly thing by its tail. "You throw it against the wall, and it sticks!"

Ross pressed the rubber gecko into my hand.

"Gee," I said. "Just what I always . . . wanted."

Ross went to the snack table for a sundae. I went to find Mary-Kate. It was time to tell my sister all about Ross's weird presents. Maybe *she* could figure out what was going on!

"First the goofy glasses, then the plant, and now a rubber gecko!" I complained to my sister. "What is up with him?"

"Maybe Ross is trying to tell you something," Mary-Kate said. "Maybe all those things are leading up to something really big."

I dangled the fake lizard in front of my face. "Like what?" I said. "Godzilla?"

Suddenly Mary-Kate pointed over my shoulder. "Ashley!" she exclaimed. "Is that Victor Nichols?"

I spun around. Victor was strutting into the rec room. He was wearing Ross's clothes and a big grin on his face.

"He looks great!" Mary-Kate said.

He sure did! He even walked differently. He looked *cool*.

"Hi, Mary-Kate," Victor said. "Hey, Ashley, those magazines and TV shows really did the trick."

"No kidding," I said.

Victor scanned the room. "Watch this!" He elbowed me, then tipped back in his seat.

"Hey, babe, you're looking hot!" he called to a girl walking by.

Mary-Kate and I exchanged a look.

"Victor!" I whispered. "Don't overdo it!"

"No worries," he replied, letting the chair come all the way back to the ground again. "So where's Kiara?"

We looked around the room. Kiara was making an ice-cream sundae at the snack table.

"Ready or not, here I come!" Victor said. He threw back his shoulders and strutted toward her.

"I think you'd better listen in," Mary-Kate said.

"I think you're right," I agreed.

I stuffed the gecko in my pocket and hurried to the snack table. I squeezed my way to the cherry vanilla and butter pecan ice-cream containers. They weren't my favorite flavors, but they got me close enough to hear Victor. I pretended to make myself a sundae.

"Hey, Kiara!" Victor said. He leaned on the table casually. "What's up?"

Kiara stopped pouring sprinkles over her ice cream.

"Oh, hi, Victor," she said. "Want an ice-cream sundae?" She held out an empty container.

Victor shook his head. "Sundaes are cool, but what really rocks is pizza," he said. "The more extreme the better—tons of anchovies, peppers, extra cheese. Know what I'm saying?"

Pizza? I wondered. *Why is Victor talking about pizza?*

Then I remembered the teen magazine. Victor must have studied Matt Clerc's pizza interview and learned it word for word!

"Onions rule," Victor went on. "But too much garlic can get kind of funky—"

"Do you like burgers?" Kiara cut in.

Silence.

"Burgers?" Victor repeated.

Kiara nodded. "I love guacamole burgers," she said. "What kind do you like?"

I snuck a peek at Victor. Tiny beads of sweat popped out on his forehead.

Come on, Victor, I thought. *Talk about burgers. Cheeseburgers, mushroom burgers—anything to do with burgers!*

"Um," Victor gulped. "Anchovy?"

Kiara wrinkled her nose. "Anchovy burgers?" she said. "I've never heard of those."

Victor opened his mouth to speak. Then he spun around and bolted from the rec room. I ran after him into the hall. He stood leaning against the wall with his eyes squeezed shut.

"You were doing great, Victor!" I said. "What happened?"

"I studied the pizza interview until I knew it by heart," Victor explained. "So when Kiara changed the subject to burgers, I choked!"

I felt bad for him. He was trying so hard. He needed a pep talk.

"You almost had a whole conversation going, Victor," I said. "That's pretty good!"

"It is?" Victor asked, opening his eyes.

"Sure!" I said. "All you need is a little more confidence and you'll be cooler than . . . ice-cream sundaes!"

"Confidence?" Victor scoffed. "How do I get that?"

"Just keep telling yourself that Kiara would be lucky to date a guy like you," I said. "It wouldn't hurt to study the most confident guys in school, too. You know—how they act, and talk, and dress."

"I can do that." Victor nodded. "There are plenty of guys like that in my dorm I can study."

"Speaking of studying," I said. "How about we start studying together for the next bio test?"

Victor stepped away from the wall and shook his head.

"I don't have time right now, Ashley," he said. "I have to get back to my dorm and start my scientific observation of the cool guys."

I stared at Victor's back as he hurried out of the building.

That's when I started to panic!

If Victor is too busy studying how to be cool, I realized, *how is he going to have time to study with me?*

Two of a Kind Diaries

Dear Diary,

The You Know Who problem just keeps getting worse!

When I bumped into Jordan behind the library late this afternoon I was happy to see him—until I remembered his secret admirer!

"You're sure you have no idea who this girl is, Jordan?" I tried again.

"I told you a hundred times, Mary-Kate," Jordan said. "I don't have a clue."

I realized I was being too hard on him. Maybe he was telling the truth. And maybe I didn't have a thing to worry about.

Diary, that's a lot of maybes!

"There's a new Morons from Mars game in the U," Jordan said. "Want to check it out?"

"I can't," I said. "I have another Heart-O-Gram to sing."

"I know, let's meet tonight in the Harrington movie room," Jordan suggested. "They're showing *Team Android* at seven-thirty. It's that flick about the baseball coach who turns his players into robots."

"That'll be great!" I exclaimed. "I'll grab the shuttle bus after dinner."

Diary, I wanted to skip all the way

to my next Heart-O-Gram assignment. Jordan and I were going to the movies together—which meant things hadn't changed between us!

Valerie was wrong, I thought. *I have seen the last of You Know Who. And so has Jordan!*

That night when I met Jordan in the Harrington movie room we picked our favorite seats near the popcorn machine.

"I'll go get us some popcorn," Jordan told me, dropping his backpack onto his seat. "Be right back."

As Jordan walked to the popcorn machine, I plopped his backpack onto the floor. A side pocket must have been open, because a note fell out. I was about to stuff it back inside, when I saw a word that made me freeze.

"P-P-Pookie!" I gasped.

My mouth hung open as I stared at the note. You Know Who had struck again!

Diary, I'm usually not a snoop. In fact, I hate snoops. But I had to read this note. I slid down in my seat and read it to myself. "Dear Pookie, Baked chocolate-chip cookies just for you. Love, M."

My eyes kept blinking as if they couldn't believe what they were reading. Not only was You Know Who back—she had an initial now. And she was baking cookies for Jordan!

Who was M? And how did she know Jordan's favorite cookies are chocolate chip?

I glanced around the room. Was You Know Who here? Now? I checked out the White Oak girls. I spotted Madelyn Sternberger. Could it be Madelyn? Or Michelle O'Neil? Melanie Monteforte?

I noticed Jordan heading back with two bags of popcorn. I quickly slid the note back into his backpack.

"I got extra butter," he said as he slid into the seat beside me.

"Sounds great." I took a bag of popcorn from him.

The movie was starting, so I decided not to mention the note.

Afterward, I didn't know how to bring it up. I didn't want to admit I'd read his personal note.

Then a bunch of his friends came over, and everyone started goofing around about the movie. So I couldn't talk to Jordan about You Know Who.

But I am going to try to find out who this mystery girl is. Don't worry, Diary, I won't get carried away.

Got to go now.

I have to flip through the yearbook and circle all the names that start with M!

Chapter 8

Monday

Dear Diary,

I learned one thing last night: There are a lot of girls at White Oak Academy whose names begin with M!

I have no choice. I have to tell Jordan I saw his note. I have to find out who this mysterious cookie-baking girl is!

I usually look forward to seeing Jordan in fencing class, but today I felt nervous. I kept glancing at the gym door for him. But the snow last night had slowed down the Harrington shuttle bus.

"Why don't you girls start warming up until the guys arrive?" Coach told us.

I turned to the girl next to me. It was Jordan's new fencing partner, Mena Morris.

"En garde!" I said, holding up my sword.

That was French for "Let's start fencing."

Mena flashed one of her famous smiles. That girl could do toothpaste ads. "You're Jordan's old partner, right?"

I nodded. There was something about "old partner" that sounded kind of depressing.

"Jordan is the best fencer," she said. She fluffed her short dark curls. "He really is!"

"He said the same about you," I said.

"He did?" Mena gasped. "Are you sure?"

I stared at Mena. She seemed awfully happy to hear that.

"Yeah," I said. "He did."

"Check us out," one of Mena's friends called to us. She and her partner did some quick fencing moves.

"Looking good, Doodles!" Mena cheered. "Way to go, Stretch!"

"Doodles? Stretch?" I said. "I thought their names are Diana and Leslie."

"Oh, they are," Mena said as she flexed her sword. "I call Diana 'Doodles' because she likes to draw. And Leslie 'Stretch' because she's tall."

She gave me a quick once-over, then smiled again. "I think I'll call you MK. That's short for Mary-Kate!"

I figured that.

Mena giggled. "I think nicknames are fun."

The door swung open, and the boys filed in. They were dressed in their fencing uniforms and carrying their gear.

"Okay," Coach called. "Let's get started!"

Mena dashed over to Jordan. I watched them laughing together about something.

Then I noticed something else. Mena kept touching Jordan's arm lightly. The way you touched a boy's arm when you want to *flirt*!

Jordan finally tore his eyes away from Mena and waved to me. I forced a smile and waved back.

TWEEEEEEET!

I jumped when Coach blew his whistle. As I lowered my fencing mask, I finally figured it out.

Mena Morris starts with an M.

Twice!

Mena likes using goofy nicknames—and Pookie is a goofy nickname!

And Mena is flirting with Jordan right now!

Diary, could Mena be You Know Who?

Dear Diary,

Is it possible to spend a whole day and night studying biology and still not get it?

I mean, if a Venus flytrap plant makes its own food, why does it have to eat insects? And is a tomato a vegetable or a fruit?

I needed Victor's help more than ever!

But what if Victor doesn't get Kiara to like him? Will he refuse to tutor me and help me pass the test?

I looked back at Kiara. Her long brown hair hung over her face as she leaned over her microscope.

Maybe Victor and Kiara aren't meant for each other, I thought. *Maybe what Victor needs is a shy, noncool girl. Someone more like he is.*

The door flew open, and Victor strutted in. He was wearing another pair of Ross's jeans and a black sweater. They looked good, like the last time he put on Ross's clothes. But this time there was something extra-different about Victor.

He oozed with *confidence*!

I watched as Victor rapped knuckles with another guy. This time he didn't miss!

Go, Victor! I thought.

Victor dropped his backpack on the floor and sat down next to me. "What's up?" he asked me.

"Who *are* you?" I teased. "And what have you done with my friend Victor?"

"It's still me," Victor assured me, smiling. "Just new and improved."

"So what happened?" I asked. I couldn't believe the change in him.

"While you were cramming biology, I was studying the cool guys in my dorm," Victor explained. "Suddenly it clicked!" He grinned. "I started talking like a cool guy, walking like a cool guy, and even eating like a cool guy!"

"*Eating* like a cool guy?" I repeated.

Victor nodded. "Instead of oatmeal this morning, I had a breakfast burrito!" he said. "Is that cool or what?"

"Oh, Victor, I'm so proud of you!" I said.

"Thanks," Victor said, ducking his head shyly. He peeked back at Kiara. "What do you think? Should I make my move now or later?"

Mr. Barber called the class to attention.

"Later," Victor decided. He leaned closer to me. "Thanks a ton, Ashley," he whispered. "You taught me so much!"

"Don't mention it," I whispered back. "But now it's time for you to teach me. Bio—remember?"

"You got it," Victor said. "Let's meet in the library at midday break. Bring your textbook and notes."

Diary, not only did my cool tips work, I have my tutor back. Now Victor will ask out Kiara, and I will get an awesome grade on the next bio test.

And *that* is the coolest thing of all!

Chapter 9

Tuesday

Dear Diary,

I had to speak to someone (besides you!) about Mena. During midday break I found Ashley in the library. She and Victor were sitting together studying their biology notes. I didn't want to interrupt, but this was an emergency!

"It *might* be Mena," Ashley said after I told her everything. "But then again, it might not."

"I hate being jealous, Ashley," I said. I placed my hands on my stomach. "It's as if something is eating me up inside. Like—"

"Mold spores?" Victor cut in.

"Huh?" I said.

"Let *me* explain!" Ashley said, her blue eyes sparkling. "When a piece of bread is moldy, it means that mold spores have landed on it. The fuzzy-looking mold spores are what eats up the bread."

"You got it!" Victor cried.

Mrs. Birnbaum, the librarian, frowned as Ashley and Victor high-fived.

"Ooooo-kay," I said. "Now that I know how mold spreads, what do I do to keep Mena from spreading onto Jordan?"

"First you have to find out if Mena really is You Know Who," Ashley said.

"How do I do that?" I asked.

"Ask her," Ashley suggested. "You're one of the Heart-O-Gram girls. You have every right to ask Mena if she sent that Heart-O-Gram."

I never thought of *that*!

"I'll do it," I decided.

My stomach tightened a little as I pictured myself talking to Mena. "Will you come with me?" I asked Ashley.

"Sorry." Ashley shook her head. "Victor and I are studying the variations of plant life."

"Go ahead, Ashley," Victor urged. "I'll go hang out at the U until you get back."

"If you're sure . . . " Ashley said.

"Go," he said, waving us away.

Ashley wrapped her scarf around her neck as we left the library. I was so happy that she was coming with me.

"Mary-Kate, did you hear what Victor said?" Ashley asked. "He's going to hang at the Student U!"

"So?" I asked. "Everybody does."

"Not Victor," Ashley explained. "He usually hangs out in the bio lab or the research library, never the U."

"He really has changed," I said. "Now let's find Mena so I can get this over with."

After asking around, we found Mena in the lounge of her dorm, Phipps House. She was just about to pop a few quarters into the snack machine.

Mena smiled when she saw Ashley and me. "Hi!" she said. "Want to share some raisins and nuts?"

Ashley and I shook our heads.

"No thanks," I said. I felt bad. *Why does Mena have to be so nice?* I thought. *Why can't she be snooty or bossy, so I could hate her?*

Ashley gave me an encouraging nod.

"Mena, I have to ask you something," I said.

"About our fencing class?" Mena asked.

"Nooooooo," I said slowly.

Mena pulled the bag of raisins and nuts out of the machine. "Then what?" she asked.

I opened my mouth, but nothing came out. Ashley gave me a sharp nudge.

"Mena, are you You Know Who?" I blurted.

Mena ripped open her snack. "You know what?" she repeated.

"Does the name Pookie ring a bell?" I asked. "How about chocolate chip-cookies?"

"Pookie?" Mena said, scrunching her eyebrows. "Chocolate-chip cookies?"

She looked totally confused, so I explained everything.

"I get it," Mena said, nodding. "You think I sent a Heart-O-Gram to Jordan."

"Well?" I demanded. "Did you?"

"I never sent a Heart-O-Gram to *any* boy," Mena said. "And I would never send one to a guy who had a girlfriend!"

"You wouldn't?" I asked.

Mena shook her head. "Jordan Marshall is a great fencer and a good friend in class," she said. "But I don't have a crush on him."

I heaved a huge sigh of relief. Ashley gave me a big grin. I knew she was happy for me, too.

Mena glanced up and down the hallway, then stepped in closer to us.

"Actually," she whispered. "The guy I really like is Peter Juarez, but he doesn't know."

I had a great idea. "Mena, why don't you send Peter a Heart-O-Gram?" I suggested. "And I'll personally sing it to him!"

Mena bit her lip, thinking it over. Then she smiled brightly. "Okay! Thanks, MK!"

"MK?" Ashley raised an eyebrow at me.

I shrugged. "My nickname."

Ashley and I left Phipps and walked across campus. My stomach felt much better now that I knew that Mena wasn't You Know Who. Until it hit me.

"I still don't know which girl sent those notes!" I declared. "Who is You Know Who?"

Ashley and I looked around the busy campus scene. There were girls everywhere.

"I don't know, Mary-Kate," Ashley admitted. "It could be anyone!"

My stomach hurt all over again.

Dear Diary,

You won't believe it, but there is more to tell you about yesterday!

After Mary-Kate and I talked to Mena, I headed to the Student U to get in some more studying time with Victor. I ran into Ross on the way.

"Hey," Ross said. He tugged the pom-pom on the top of my wool hat. "I was looking all over for you!"

I was about to ask why when he reached into his pocket and handed me a CD.

"The Wonder of . . . Whale Sounds?" I asked, reading the cover. "What kind of music is this?"

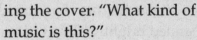

"Okay, so it's not the hottest new group." Ross chuckled. "But whale sounds are great to relax to."

Heart to Heart

I stared at the CD. Was it another part of Ross's Valentine surprise?

"Ross?" I said. "Are you trying to tell me something with these . . . unusual presents?"

Ross didn't answer me. Instead, he suddenly spun around. A big clump of snow clung to the back of his parka. I spotted several of Ross's friends laughing and waving snowballs at him.

"You're not getting away with that!" Ross laughed. He knelt down and scooped up a handful of snow.

I decided to get out of there before I got caught in a major snowball fight.

Oh well, I thought, slipping the CD into my parka pocket. *Whales are more romantic than goofy sunglasses. And rubber lizards. I think.*

As soon as I stepped inside the Student Union, I forgot all about whales and Valentine's Day. Victor and a group of older kids were standing around the sound system. Techno music blared from the speakers, and Victor was bopping a bit with the beat!

"Hey, isn't that the bio-head from Harrington?" I heard a girl shout over the music.

"Yeah," another girl shouted back. "He's like this whole new person now!"

The boy in charge of the music pulled out a CD and handed it to Victor.

"Thanks for the heads-up on the tunes," the guy said.

"No prob, dude," Victor said. "Happy to be of help."

My jaw dropped. Most *First* Formers ignored Victor. Now he was giving music advice to the older kids?

Victor crossed to a mirror. I hurried over to him.

"Hey, Ashley," Victor said, running his hand through his hair. "How would I look with blond tips?"

Blond tips? Victor? I was so stunned, I couldn't even answer.

A trio of girls strolled by and glanced at him.

"Ladies . . . " Victor said. He winked at them, and they all started giggling.

I started gagging!

Victor had done his homework, Diary. A little too well!

"Okay, Victor," I said. "How about we get back to the variations of plant life."

"No can do," Victor said. "The guys asked me to snowboard before the break is up. I'm sure I can nail it now."

"How about after school?" I asked.

"Sorry," Victor said. He pointed to the older boy

by the CD player. "That's Jeffy Jeff, the Harrington DJ. He said he'd show me how to master the mix."

"Master the mix?" I repeated.

"Spin discs!" Victor rolled his eyes. "Get with it, Ashley!"

"Get with it?" I squeaked. *"You're* telling *me* to get with it?"

The door opened, and Kiara walked in. She was with her friends Alyssa and Jolene.

"Ashley, watch this!" Victor whispered.

He cupped his hands around his mouth. "Kiara!" he shouted. "You've just been voted prettiest girl in the U. And the prize is *me!"*

Kiara stared at Victor. So did her friends. I could tell she didn't think Victor was very funny.

I didn't, either.

Kiara never looked our way again before she hurried out of the U.

Diary, all I'd wanted to do was help make Victor cool. Instead, I'd created a monster!

Chapter 10

Friday

Dear Diary,

Valentine's Day is just one day  away! I even drew a big red heart on my calendar right around February 14 (not that I would forget!).

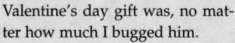
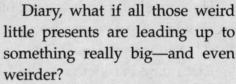

Ross still wouldn't tell me what my real Valentine's day gift was, no matter how much I bugged him.

Diary, what if all those weird little presents are leading up to something really big—and even weirder?

Today during lunch period I walked Ross to the Harrington shuttle bus. I was on my way to the *Acorn* office. I had promised to help Phoebe sort Heart-O-Grams. I felt bad that I hadn't been more involved.

"I ran into Victor on the bus today," Ross told me. "He's turning out to be one cool dude."

Too cool, if you ask me, Diary.

I shrugged. "It's what Victor wanted," I said. "Now he finally feels cool enough to ask Kiara out for Valentine's Day."

"Has he asked her yet?" Ross asked.

"Maybe," I replied. "He told me in bio that he was going to ask her the next time he saw her."

The shuttle bus pulled up.

"Got to run," Ross said. "But look in your backpack. Front pocket."

"For what?" I asked, digging into my pack.

"You'll see," Ross teased.

I felt something rough and hard. Was it a rose quartz crystal? That would be romantic!

I pulled out a jagged black rock.

"Ross?" I asked. "You gave me a rock for Valentine's Day?"

"It's another part of your Valentine's Day present," Ross said. "This one says it all!"

I stared at the rock as Ross ran for the bus. *This says it all? What does it say?*

I was so confused. I stuffed the rock in my backpack and made my way to the *Acorn* office. Phoebe and Fiona were already there.

Mary-Kate came in, still wearing her Heart-O-Gram costume.

"How'd it go?" Phoebe asked.

Mary-Kate shrugged her shoulders. "It's hard to sing Heart-O-Grams when your own heart is sinking," she grumbled.

"What do you mean?" I asked her.

"It's one day before Valentine's Day," Mary-Kate

said, pulling off her giant cardboard heart. "And I still don't know who Jordan's secret admirer is."

I sat down on a chair next to Mary-Kate.

"You think you have problems." I groaned. "Ross just gave me a rock for Valentine's Day. And it's not a diamond."

"Excuse me."

I glanced up. Kiara stood in the doorway.

"Hi, Kiara," I said. "What's up?"

She placed her hands on her hips. "I want to take back my Heart-O-Gram!" she announced.

We all stared at her.

"What Heart-O-Gram?" I asked.

Kiara strode into the room. "Last week I ordered a gram for a guy I liked," she explained. "But I've changed my mind."

Did I just hear right? I thought. *Is there a Harrington boy that Kiara has a crush on? Was Victor totally out of the running from day one? Poor Victor—he tried so hard and never even had a chance.*

"I never got a confirmation e-mail," Kiara said. "So I know he never got it."

"Then it's probably still in the basket," Phoebe said as she walked toward her desk. "What's the boy's name?"

"Victor," Kiara answered. "Victor Nichols."

Heart to Heart

"Victor?" I gasped.

"No way!" Mary-Kate murmured.

"You mean . . . you like him?" I asked.

"I used to," Kiara corrected. "I liked his smile, his intelligence, even how shy he acted all the time."

Diary, I couldn't believe my ears. All this time Kiara liked Victor. And no one—not even Victor—had a clue!

"I don't get it, Kiara," I said. "If you like Victor so much, why do you want to take back your Heart-O-Gram?"

"Because lately Victor has been acting so goofy!" Kiara complained. "It's like he's trying to be cool like all the other guys in school!"

"What's wrong with that?" I asked.

"Cool isn't important to me," Kiara said. "I like brainy, down-to-earth guys."

Now she tells me! I thought.

All this time Kiara liked the old Victor. But thanks to me, the old Victor was history!

"Kiara, I found it!" Phoebe waved a form in the air. "It must have fallen on the floor. I'm sorry."

"It's okay," Kiara said. She looked relieved. "At least it didn't go out."

Phoebe showed me the form. It was dated right

around the time I'd started changing Victor—for the *worse*!

I had to fix this somehow!

"Kiara, it's my fault," I confessed. "I tried to turn Victor into a cool guy because he likes you, too."

Kiara looked totally surprised. "He does?" she asked.

I nodded. "He thought being cool was the only way you would like him," I explained. "*Really* like him!"

"But I don't like the way he is now!" Kiara said.

"Don't worry," I said. "The minute Victor finds out you liked him the old way, he'll go back to being his good old self. I know it!"

"How am I going to tell him?" Kiara asked.

"I'll take care of that," Mary-Kate said, slipping her cardboard heart back over her head.

"I know exactly what the message should say!" I scribbled a note and handed it to Fiona. Mary-Kate joined her at the keyboard.

Mary-Kate grinned as she read the message I wrote. She turned to Fiona. "Hit it, Fiona!" she ordered.

Fiona played a fancy string of notes as an intro, then Mary-Kate sang the new Heart-O-Gram.

"Victor, you didn't have to

change a thing," she sang. "You always made my heart go—zing!"

I smiled at Kiara. "I think he'll get the message," I said.

"I think so, too!" Kiara said, smiling back.

Do you believe it, Diary?

Victor never needed a makeover to begin with!

Which only proves—the best person to be is yourself!

Dear Diary,

Do you believe it, Diary? It's Valentine's Day Eve, and we had finally sung our last Heart-O-Grams!

"I don't think I ever want to hear another love song as long as I live!" Cheryl groaned.

Cheryl, Elise, Valerie, and I were still wearing our costumes as we dragged ourselves to the TV room. We were too tired to take them off. Our plan was to hang out in front of the TV for the rest of the night.

"My feet are killing me." Elise moaned. "From now on I'm wearing nothing but sneakers!"

"I think I lost my voice," Valerie croaked. "How can I be a musical theater star without my voice?"

"We really did go all out for this project," I said.

I opened the door to the TV room.

"Surprise!" Phoebe shouted.

The room was filled with kids. They all applauded as we filed in.

"What's this all about?" I asked.

Everyone stepped aside—and there was a brand-new DVD player!

"I picked it up this afternoon," Phoebe said. "We have all of you to thank!"

Team Heart-O-Gram took a bow. I spotted Jordan standing in the back, so I went to join him.

"I haven't seen you in a while," Jordan said. "You're not upset about that Heart-O-Gram, are you?"

I still wasn't thrilled, but Jordan looked too cute in his Cubs jersey for me to be upset.

"Does this answer your question?" I put my arms around his waist and gave him a big hug.

"I'm glad," Jordan said. "Because tomorrow is Valentine's Day. Do you want to go into town and have some fun?"

"It's a date!" I declared.

"Oh, wow," Jordan said, snapping his fingers. "I just remembered something."

"What?" I asked.

"Today's my mom's birthday," Jordan said. "I forgot to call her."

There was a pay phone hanging on the wall.

Heart to Heart

Jordan called his mom while I poured myself a cup of hot chocolate from the cocoa machine.

"Hi, Mom, it's me!" I heard Jordan say. "Happy birthday!"

I grabbed a can of Whippy Whip cream and began squirting some into my cocoa cup. Then I heard Jordan groan.

"Aw, Mom," he whispered. "I told you not to call me Pookie!"

"Pookie?" I cried.

Jordan glanced my way. He hung up and ran over to me. "Mary-Kate!" he exclaimed. "Take your finger off the can. Take your finger off the can!"

"Huh?" I said. I looked down and gasped. My cocoa cup was overflowing with Whippy Whip! I was so distracted by Jordan that I forgot to take my finger off the squirter!

"Whoops," I said. I quickly mopped up the mess.

"Your mom calls you Pookie?" I asked Jordan. "Pookie?"

Jordan blushed. "She's called me that since I was about three years old," he said. "I wish she'd stop."

"Jordan," I said. "The person who sent you the Heart-O-Gram called you Pookie. But I couldn't get myself to say it."

"Pookie?" Jordan said. "No way!"

It didn't make sense to me, either. How did Jordan's mom get a Heart-O-Gram form? Unless . . .

"Jordan, did you send your mom the last copy of the *White Oak Acorn*?" I asked.

Jordan shook his head. "No," he said. "I just faxed her the article about my fencing championship."

The article! I remembered. *The article with the Heart-O-Gram form on the same page!*

"Did your mom also send you cookies?" I asked Jordan. "Chocolate-chip cookies—along with a note?"

"Yup," Jordan said. "But—"

"And she signed the note 'M'?" I cut in.

"Yeah. M for Mom," Jordan said. "Mary-Kate, where are you going with all this?"

Diary, I wanted to do cartwheels all around campus. I finally found out who You Know Who was—and it was not some girl at school with a crush on Jordan!

"Jordan!" I squealed, jumping up and down. "That's who sent you the mystery Heart-O-Gram. Your *mom*!"

Jordan turned red as everyone stared at him.

"Thanks a lot, Mary-Kate," he grumbled. Luckily, he was smiling when he said it, so I knew he wasn't mad.

"Whoops!" I giggled.

Now I don't have to worry about some other girl at school trying to steal my boyfriend anymore. Everything is great between us.

And, Diary, the timing couldn't be better.

Valentine's Day, here I come!

Chapter 11

Saturday

Dear Diary,

Diary, my first Valentine's Day with my first boyfriend gets an A+!

Jordan and I took the van to town. We went to this great new sports restaurant called Cleats and ate cheeseburgers and buffalo wings. Then we gave each other presents.

I gave Jordan a book on famous fencing scenes in the movies. He thought it was awesome.

Jordan gave me a Sammy Sosa bobble-head doll. So cute!

"That's not all," Jordan said. He pulled a heart-shaped box of chocolates out of his backpack and gave it to me.

"I love it!" I said.

"You don't think it's too corny?" Jordan asked. "I mean, the heart-shaped box and all?"

"It's perfect!"

That's right, Diary. I am now a fan of the heart-shaped box!

On the van ride home, Jordan and I took a bite out of each chocolate in the box. How else would we know what was inside?

Then we did something that was way more

important than any Valentine's Day gift: We made a promise to always tell each other everything. That way, there would be no more worrying over anything.

I also made Jordan one more promise.

"I'll never call you Pookie," I said. "No matter what!"

"Phew!" Jordan said. "That's a relief!"

"Which means," I said slowly, "I'll have to think of something else. Like Shmoopie . . . or Bunnykins . . . or Sweetums!"

"Arrrgh!" Jordan groaned.

On the other hand, Diary, maybe I'll just call him Jordan!

Dear Diary,

Guess how I spent the first few hours of Valentine's Day. Give up?

Taking a biology test!

No, not *the* biology test. That's in another two weeks. This was a test in the back of a bio workbook that Victor gave to me after we studied together last night.

He got Kiara's Heart-O-Gram just a few hours earlier and, boy, was he psyched. He was also glad to be his old self again!

"I really hated snowboarding," Victor confessed.

"And talking cool made me feel like a jerk. And I didn't want to have to keep putting goop in my hair. And—"

"I get the idea." I giggled. "Welcome back, Victor!"

So this morning while Victor and Kiara were planning their Valentine's Day date, I had a date with Victor's biology workbook.

"'Multiple choice,'" I read to myself. "'Which of the following foods does not come from a seed? A) Coffee B) Honey C) Chocolate.'"

I circled B. Honey was made by bees from the nectar of flowers.

Next question.

"'True or false? An amoeba is a three-celled animal.'"

That was easy.

"False," I said. Amoebas have one cell.

After answering all the questions, I counted up my score. Then I turned the page for my grade and my eyes popped wide open!

"A minus!" I shrieked. "I got an A minus!"

The other kids looked up from their books. Mrs. Birnbaum pressed her finger to her lips.

"Sorry," I said, still smiling.

I pulled on my parka, scooped up my books, and left the library. I wanted to show my score to Phoebe, and Mary-Kate, and Ross—

Heart to Heart

"Ross," I murmured. *I wonder how he wants to spend Valentine's Day*, I thought. *We never did make any plans.*

I hoped there wouldn't be any weird presents involved!

I practically ran all the way to Porter House. When I opened the door, I saw Phoebe standing by the staircase.

"Phoebe, guess what?" I said.

Phoebe didn't answer. She gazed at me with a sly grin on her face.

A bunch of girls from the dorm sat on the stairs behind her. They were grinning at me, too!

"Okay, everybody," I said. "What's up?"

No one said a word. They just pointed to a sign on the Porter House lounge.

"'Aloha, Ashley'?" I read out loud. I glanced back at them, puzzled. "I don't get it."

"What are you waiting for?" Phoebe asked. "Go in!"

I shrugged as I opened the lounge door.

"Oh . . . my . . . gosh!" I said.

I dropped my backpack on the floor and stepped farther inside.

The whole room was decorated with paper palm trees, plastic hibiscus flowers, and posters of the Hawaiian Islands. Flowered leis were hanging everywhere. In the back a table was decked with a

grass-style tablecloth and was covered with papayas, coconuts, and pineapples. There were tall glasses filled with fruit smoothies and bowls of macadamia nuts. There was even a pineapple pizza!

Soft music began filling the room—Hawaiian ukulele music!

"Aloha!" a voice said.

I spun around. Ross was walking into the room holding a beautiful lei. The flowers smelled amazing!

"Happy Valentine's Day, Ashley," Ross said.

I was so surprised, I couldn't speak. Ross helped me off with my jacket like a real gentleman. He draped the lei around my neck.

"Ross?" I finally managed to say. "What's going on?"

"I couldn't get you a plane ticket to Hawaii," Ross said. "So I hope this is the next best thing."

It all started to make sense!

"That's why you gave me the goofy sunglasses and that rubber gecko, and that CD of whale sounds," I said. "But what was the deal with the black rock?"

"It's a volcanic lava rock from Oahu," Ross explained. "And that plant you're growing is a Hawaiian ti plant. I got them both on-line."

That's what the presents were all about—they were clues leading up to Ross's Hawaiian luau.

"Ross Lambert!" I said. "You *are* romantic!"

I heard the others giggle as I gave Ross a kiss. They were crowding the doorway.

"Does that mean you like it?" Ross asked.

"It's perfect!" I declared. "Except for one thing."

Ross looked worried. "What?" he asked.

"The pineapple pizza." I smiled and wrinkled my nose. "I'd rather have pepperoni and extra cheese."

Then I remembered something in my backpack. My Valentine's Day present for Ross.

"Happy Valentine's Day!" I said as I gave him the disc of romantic songs.

"Thanks," Ross said. "Let's play it."

"I have a better idea!" I grabbed a lei draped over a lamp. Then I hung it around Ross's neck. "Let's hula!"

"Hula?" Ross cried. "I don't think—"

"Come on, Lambert." I started swaying my arms and hips. "You can do it!"

Everyone piled into the lounge for a real Valentine's Day luau. And guess who showed up?

Two of a Kind Diaries

Mary-Kate and Jordan, and Victor and Kiara!

Diary, this was the best Valentine's Day surprise I ever got.

And for Mary-Kate and me—the best Valentine's Day ever!

Dear Diary,

I had the best idea for our Prom Princess video!

I swiveled my desk chair to face Phoebe. "We'll video the other girls getting signatures with my voice explaining the contest rules," I said. "We'll end that part when I decide to run for Prom Princess."

"I love it!" Phoebe beamed.

"Next we'll tape me collecting signatures," I said.

"We need to get some signatures at breakfast." Phoebe said. "Everyone else has a major head start. Even Dana!"

We left the room and ran into Tammi Patterson coming down the hall. Phoebe stood back with the camera running.

"Hi, Tammi!" I said. "I just decided to run for Prom Princess. Will you sign my form?"

"You'd be perfect, Ashley," Tammi said. "But I signed Dana's form last night."

"Oh." I tried not to look disappointed.

"I'm really sorry, Ashley." Tammi pointed toward Layne Wagner and Carmen Barnes. "Maybe they'll sign for you."

"Thanks." I hurried over to Layne and Carmen. Phoebe jogged after me with the camera. "Hi, guys!"

"Hey, Ashley!" Carmen smiled. "What's up?"

"I decided to run for Prom Princess," I said. "Will you sign my form?"

"I can't," Layne said. "I voted for Lavender."

"Me, too," Carmen said.

"I understand," I said. Both girls were good friends with Lavender Duncan. "See you later."

Phoebe and I waited until they were gone.

"Don't worry, Ashley," Phoebe said. "I know for a fact that Summer and Elise haven't signed yet."

I was glad to hear that, but Summer Sorenson and Elise Van Hook were only two people.

That's why I'm worried, Diary. What if everyone I know has already nominated someone else for Prom Princess? Is it too late?

WIN A TRIP

to the **World Premiere** of
Mary-Kate and Ashley's
new movie...
NEW YORK MINUTE!

Mail to: **MARY-KATE AND ASHLEY**
NEW YORK MINUTE PREMIERE
c/o HarperEntertainment
Attention: Children's Marketing Department
10 East 53rd Street, New York, NY 10022

No purchase necessary.

Name: _____

Address: _____

City: _____ State: _____ Zip: _____

Phone: _____ Age: _____

⬛ HarperEntertainment
An Imprint of HarperCollinsPublishers
www.harpercollins.com

Mary-Kate and Ashley *NEW YORK MINUTE*
"Win A Trip to the Movie Premiere" Sweepstakes

OFFICIAL RULES:

1. NO PURCHASE OR PAYMENT NECESSARY TO ENTER OR WIN.

2. **How to Enter.** To enter the *New York Minute* Movie Premiere Sweepstakes ("Sweepstakes") complete the official entry form or hand print your name, address, age and phone number along with the words "*New York Minute* Movie Premiere Sweepstakes" on a 3" x 5" card and mail to: Sweepstakes, c/o HarperEntertainment, Attn: Children's Marketing Department, 10 East 53rd Street, New York, NY 10022. Entries must be received no later than March 15, 2004. Enter as often as you wish, but each entry must be mailed separately. One entry per envelope. Partially completed, illegible, or mechanically reproduced entries will not be accepted. HarperCollins Publishers, Inc. (hereinafter "HarperCollins" or "Sponsor") is not responsible for lost, late, mutilated, illegible, stolen, postage due, incomplete, or misdirected entries. All entries become the property of Dualstar Entertainment Group, LLC, and will not be returned.

3. **Eligibility.** Sweepstakes open to all legal residents of the United States, (excluding Colorado and Rhode Island), who are between the ages of five and fifteen on March 15, 2004. HarperCollins Publishers, Inc. ("HarperCollins"), Time Warner ("Warner"), Parachute Properties and Parachute Press, Inc. ("Parachute"), Dualstar Entertainment Group, LLC, ("Dualstar"), and their respective parent companies, trustees, subsidiaries, franchisees, affiliates, licensees, distributors, divisions, directors, officers, shareholders, employees, agents, independent contractors, attorneys, representatives, and advertising, promotion and fulfillment agencies (collectively, the "Participating Entities"), and their immediate families (parents, children, siblings, spouse) and persons with whom each of the above are domiciled are not eligible to participate in this promotion. **Offer void where prohibited or restricted by law.**

4. **Odds of Winning.** Odds of winning depend on the total number of entries received. Approximately 750,000 sweepstakes announcements published. All prizes will be awarded. Winner will be randomly drawn on or about March 30, 2004, by HarperCollins, whose decisions are final. Potential winner will be notified by mail and will be required to sign and return an affidavit of eligibility and release of liability within 14 days of notification. Failure to do so will result in forfeiture of prize and the selection of another winner by random drawing. Prize won by minors will be awarded to parent or legal guardian who must sign and return all required legal documents. By entry and acceptance of their prize, winners and their parent or legal guardians consent to the use of their names, photographs, likeness, statements, voice, voice likeness, city and state address and biographical information by the Participating Entities on a worldwide basis and in all forms of media without further compensation, except where prohibited.

5. **Grand Prize.** One (1) Grand Prize Winner will receive a trip to the movie premiere of "*New York Minute*." HarperCollins reserves the right at its sole discretion to substitute another prize of equal or of greater value in the event prize is unavailable. All expenses not stated are the winner's sole expense.

6. **Trip Details.** HarperCollins will provide the Sweepstakes winner and one parent or legal guardian with round-trip coach air transportation from the major airport nearest winner to the movie premiere's city and standard hotel accommodations for a two-night stay, ground transportation to and from hotel to movie premiere, and a Mary-Kate and Ashley gift bag. Accommodations are room and tax only. Winner and traveling companion are responsible for all incidentals and all other charges, except the hotel tax, including but not limited to meals, gratuities, all other taxes and transfers. Winner must be available to travel any days and nights between April 1, 2004 and May 31, 2004, or other dates to coincide with the movie premiere. Airline, hotel, and other travel arrangements will be made by HarperCollins in its discretion. HarperCollins reserves the right, in its sole discretion, to substitute an alternate trip or a cash payment of $2000.00 for the Grand Prize. Travel, premiere tickets and use of hotel are at risk of winner and HarperCollins does not assume any liability. Certain blackout dates and other restrictions apply. Approximate retail value is $2000.00.

7. **Prize Limitations.** Prize will be awarded. Prize is non-transferable and cannot be sold or redeemed for cash except as specified above at Sponsor's sole discretion. Any and all federal, state, or local taxes are fully and solely the responsibility of the winner.

8. **Additional Terms.** Additional terms: By entering, entrants and winners agree a) to the official rules and decisions of the judges, which will be final in all respects, and to waive any claim to ambiguity of the official rules; and b) to release, discharge, indemnify and hold harmless the Participating Entities from and against any and all claims, liability or damages due to any injuries, damages, or losses to any person (including death) or property of any kind resulting in whole or in part, directly or indirectly, from acceptance, possession, use, or misuse of any prize received in this Sweepstakes or any participation in this Sweepstakes.

9. **Use of Entrants' Information.** HarperCollins may only use the personally identifiable information obtained from the entrants in accordance with its privacy policy, which may be found at http://www.harperchildrens.com/hch/parents/privacy/.

10. **Dispute Resolution.** Any dispute arising from this Sweepstakes will be determined according to the laws of the State of New York, without reference to its conflict of law principles, and the entrants consent to the personal jurisdiction of the State and Federal courts located in New York County and agree that such courts have exclusive jurisdiction over all such disputes.

11. **Winner Information.** To obtain the name of the winner, please send your request and a self-addressed stamped envelope (residents of Vermont may omit return postage) to "*New York Minute* Movie Premiere Sweepstakes Winners", c/o HarperEntertainment, 10 East 53rd Street, New York, NY 10022 by July 1, 2004.

12. Sweepstakes Sponsor: HarperCollins Publishers, Inc.

Mary-Kate
as Misty

Ashley
as Amber

Let's go
save the world...
again!

MARY-KATE AND ASHLEY
in ACTION!

only on

TOON
Disney
CHANNEL

Call your cable operator
or satellite provider
to request Toon Disney.

DUALSTAR
ANIMATION
©2003 Dualstar Entertainment Group, LLC

ToonDisney.com ©Disney

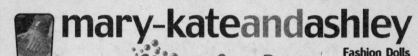

mary-kateandashley

Fashion Dolls

 *Super Spa Day*™

Spend a day at the spa with
Mary-Kate and Ashley! you can give
them manicures and pedicures...

...and change their
makeup for a
fun night out!

① Soak their hands
and feet in water

② to reveal their
favorite nail color!

③ Use the applicator to change
thier eye makeup and lip colors
for a dramatic new look.

Transform their
cool spa chair
into beautiful
vanity mirrors.

**Look for the new
Mary-Kate and Ashley Dolls,
Coming Soon!**

 Real **Dolls**
for **Real**
Girls

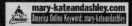 **mary-kateandashley.com**
America Online Keyword: mary-kateandashley

 DUALSTAR

 MATTEL